D1472831

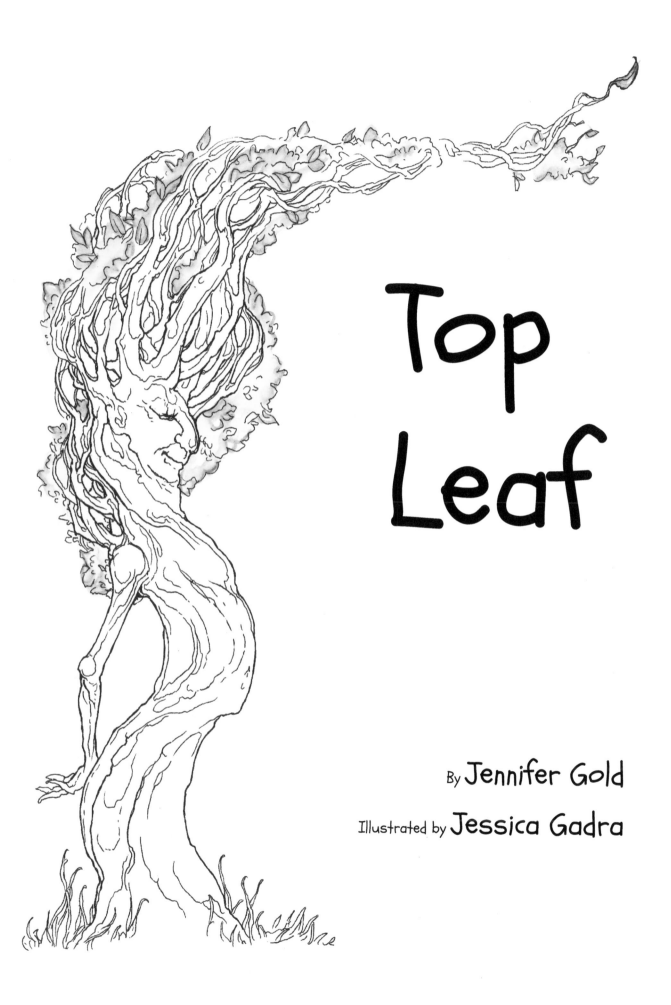

Top Leaf

By Jennifer Gold

Illustrated by Jessica Gadra

Buffalo Arts Publishing

For information, address Buffalo Arts Publishing,
179 Greenfield Drive, Tonawanda, NY 14150

Email: info@buffaloartspublishing.com

Cover and inside illustrations by Jessica Gadra

ISBN 978-0-9978741-3-6

Acknowledgements

Thank you for all the helpful critiquing and constant support from the talented women in my poetry group. They have been meeting every month for over thirty years and still can't decide on a name.

To **Highlights Foundation** for their *Everything you Need to Know About Children's Book Publishing: Crash Course 2017*.

To **Burdick's Blueberry Farm** in East Otto, NY, where the idea first sprouted.

To **Jack Jamieson** for his help in the initial editing and layout.

To **Len Kagelmacher** – Proprietor of Buffalo Arts Publishing, for his friendly and professional advice.

And above all, thank you to **Jessica Gadra** for her utterly charming illustrations.

Jennifer Gold, 2017

To Helen,
who always encouraged me
to write.

From the first day
of spring, just after
unfurling himself
from his bud, the leaf
talked loudly
about how important
he was because
he lived right on the top
of the old tree.

He said he could see
for miles and miles
and *miles*.

1

"What can you see today?" called a leaf
in the middle of the tree.

"I can see the children going to school," he said,
making his voice sound important.

"And there is smoke in the distance. Perhaps
there is a fire in the woods."

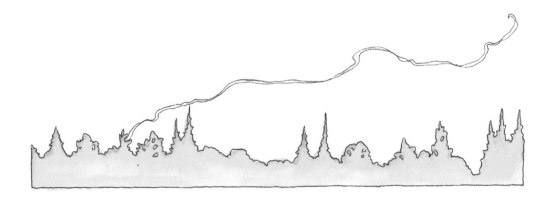

All the leaves chattered together.

Some of them twisted around
on their stalks trying to see
what the leaf could see.

But they were not high enough.

3

Sometimes the leaf was VERY rude.

"I'm not in the mood to talk. Don't bother me!" he said

"You must wait until I am ready to tell you what is happening."

Then he said, "From now on you must call me Top Leaf."

A small green leaf hanging
just below Top Leaf
called up to him.

"Hey! You're only at the top by chance.
What makes you think you're so special?"

Top Leaf didn't answer.

"You need us too," she said. "You'd look pretty silly
up there all by yourself!" And she laughed.

"NONSENSE!" shouted Top Leaf. "I don't need
any of you! I'm the greatest so BE QUIET!"

One day he shouted at a squirrel:

"GET OFF MY BRANCH!
You are too heavy and you are making me lower than the others!

That is NOT where I am supposed to be!"

"Oh my!" said the squirrel with a giggle as she scampered away.

So the leaves stopped asking Top Leaf questions.

In fact they stopped talking to him at all.

Top Leaf pretended he didn't mind. He would swing around on his stalk shouting,

"Ooooh!" and "Aaaah!"
hoping to get the leaves to ask him questions.

But they didn't.

And he was lonely.

Top Leaf soon got bored, so he made up a song.
He sang in a high, squeaky voice:

"I'm on top of a very big tree,
    I own everything I can see.
You down there are really small,
    You don't matter -- NOT AT ALL!"

And then he'd laugh and dance around on his
stalk with delight.

The old tree had never known a leaf to be
so rude.

She asked the animals what to do.

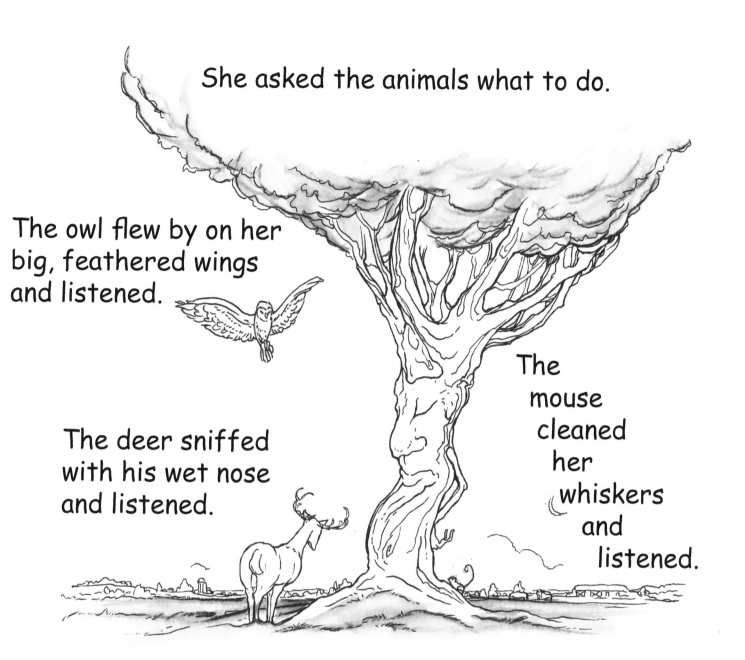

The owl flew by on her big, feathered wings and listened.

The mouse cleaned her whiskers and listened.

The deer sniffed with his wet nose and listened.

"He'll learn by the fall," they said.

"Yes," said the tree, "He certainly will."

Summer came and so did the people from the village.

They sat on the grass and had picnics in the shade of the old tree.

Children climbed the branches. The old tree liked that.

Some rough children pulled leaves off and threw them on the ground. The old tree didn't like that. Neither did the leaves.

By the end of September the days
were warm and the nights were cold.

The leaves started to change color.

The green was disappearing but the leaves
were still pretty in their bright reds,
golden yellows and rusty browns.

"I don't feel the same," said Top Leaf
one crisp October day.
"It's Fall," said the old tree.
"Look around."
"No!" said Top Leaf in a
frightened voice.
"I don't want to fall."

"You'll be fine," said the old tree.
"You won't get hurt."

"But I'll be in a pile with all the others. I won't
be important anymore," whispered
Top Leaf.

"You have to go sometime," repeated the old tree kindly.

"Just let go."

Top Leaf was silent.

"You might be a nest for an animal," said the old tree, "or crumble into compost and make the ground rich for plants."

"STOP TALKING ABOUT IT!" said Top Leaf, hanging on grimly in a strong gust of wind.

Then he looked down at the small leaf
who had talked to him in the spring.

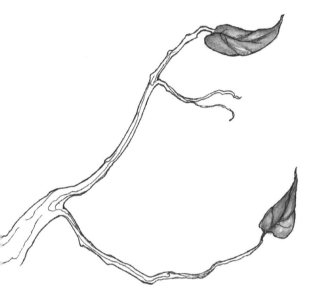

She was still on her twig.

"HEY YOU!" Top Leaf shouted,
"Are you going?"

"Yes, of course I'm going!"
she said.

The wind blew again and Top Leaf gulped as he
felt himself coming loose.

"Ummm, hey leaf! Could we go together?"

When there was no answer he said very quietly,
"Can we go together? I'm scared."

"We can start out together," said the small leaf, hiding a smile, "but once we are over that hill I'm going where the wind blows!"

"Really?" said Top Leaf.

"Yes, my very own adventure. It's so exciting!" said the small leaf.

The old tree swayed her branches again.

"Ready?" called the small leaf.

"OK," said Top Leaf bravely, and he let go.

"Ooooh! This is great!" said Top Leaf
laughing as the wind lifted him off
his twig and out into the meadow.

The small leaf twirled happily around him.
"You're not *Nasty Leaf* anymore," she said.
"You're just leaf. I'm glad I waited for you."

That was a surprise for the top leaf.
He hadn't known that the other
leaves had called him "nasty."

He had been sad and lonely.
         Now he had a friend.
                  He was happy.

As they tumbled away across the field, the old tree heard their laughter getting

fainter

and

fainter.

She smiled.
All her leaves had gone.
She was ready for winter
and a nice, long rest.

It began to snow.

Author's Note: With very few props, this story could easily be adapted into a play for 5-6 year-olds.

- JG

CPSIA information can be obtained
at www.ICGtesting.com
Printed in the USA
LVHW07n1511060718
582924LV00013B/118/P